The Number 7 Shirt

by

Alan Gibbons

Illustrated by Aleksandar Sotirovski

To the Flowers of Manchester, Munich '58

First published in 2008 in Great Britain by
Barrington Stoke Ltd
18 Walker Street, Edinburgh, EH3 7LP

www.barringtonstoke.co.uk

This edition first published 2012

ISBN: 978-1-78112-133-7

Printed in China by Leo

Contents

Chapter 1
Jimmy and George

I'm Jimmy Beech. I want to be a footballer. This is my story.

Let me show you my scrap-book. It's got the reports and photos from all my matches. See that photo on the front page? North Park Juniors was my first team. I was playing for them when the scout came from Manchester United. That's me in the number seven shirt.

Don't laugh. I know the haircut is a bit odd. But I was only nine when it was taken. Mum took me to get my hair cut. I'm fourteen now. I get my own hair cut these days.

I scored four times the day the scout came. His name was Mark. We all knew who he was. Everyone wanted to do well. This was Manchester United. Clubs don't come bigger than that.

Man U's always been part of my life. For as long as I can remember. My dad's a fan. So's my mum. Even my sister loves Man U and she's weird. She's a Goth and she looks like a vampire.

There's posters of all the Man U players all over my room. I've even got the ones from the old days. My favourite players are the ones who wore the number seven shirt for United – Georgie Best, Bryan Robson, Eric Cantona, David Beckham, Cristiano Ronaldo. They're my heroes.

You'll think this is stupid, but I talk to them. I'll pretend I can really see them. It's as if they're standing right in front of me. Sometimes it feels as if they're talking back to me. I ask them to give me advice, most of all when things aren't going well.

Things didn't start too well the day Mark came to see me play for the first time. Mark's the scout for Man U – remember? I was so excited I could hardly move. My legs felt like jelly. Every time I got the ball it ran away from me. Every time I tried to shoot it got stuck under my feet and I almost tripped over. Even when I did get a shot on target, it was really soft. It just rolled into the keeper's hands.

I started to lose my temper. I used to do that when things were going badly. I got angry with myself. Then I started to get angry with everyone else. I saw Dad shake his head. If I carried on like this, our coach would take me off.

I had to do something. So, like I just said I pretended one of those old Man U players was right there next to me. So I talked to Georgie. That's Georgie Best.

George told me to forget about the scout.
He told me to show what I could do.

The next time I got the ball, I did what he
said. I kept my eye on the ball. I didn't look
at Mark. I didn't look at Dad. My mind was on
the game and nothing else. I weaved this way.
I weaved that way. I made space for myself.
When I saw the goal between two defenders, I
shot. The ball hit the net. Sweet!

I scored three more times after that. The
best one was when my best mate Carl rolled

the ball into the box. I leaned forward and kept my head down. Then I struck the ball with the inside of my foot. It flew past the keeper like a bullet and the net rippled.

Mark went over to Dad at the end of the match. He asked if I wanted to go for a trial.

It worked, George. The scout's asked me to go for a trial.

George Best
The Belfast Boy

⚽ Pele said that George was the greatest footballer in the world. Maradona also thought he was one of the world's greats.

⚽ George was born on May 22nd, 1946 in East Belfast.

⚽ When Bob Bishop, the Manchester United scout in Belfast, saw George he sent the United manager Matt Busby a telegram. It said: "I've found you a genius."

⚽ In six seasons George Best scored 115 goals in 290 games. United won the Championship twice.

 ⚽ When Man U beat Benfica of Portugal 5–1 away from home in the European Cup, George came back wearing a sombrero hat. The newspapers called him 'El Beatle'.

'El' means 'the' in Spanish and they called him 'El Beatle' because now he was as great as the Beatles, the world's most famous pop group.

⚽ In 1968 Manchester United beat Benfica 4–1 again. George scored one of the goals.

⚽ The same year he was voted European Player of the year.

⚽ Sadly, George started to drink heavily and his career at United ended when he was only 26.

⚽ George said of himself, "When I'm gone people will forget all the rubbish and all they'll remember will be the football. That'll do for me."

Chapter 2
The Trials

There were 30 kids at the first trial.
It lasted an hour. We practised skills and
technique. Then we played a few five-a-side
games. I did OK but so did the other boys. Some
of them were really good. I was always the best
player for North Park. I wasn't the best player
here. These boys were the best from all the
junior teams. There was a lot of competition
and I was getting worried. What if Mark sent
me home? What if I wasn't good enough?

After I got dressed I waited to hear how it went. Dad came over. He had a smile as big as a banana.

"You did well," he said. "They want you back next week."

That night I could hardly sleep. I tossed and turned for hours. In the end I turned the light on and looked at the posters of all my favourite players. I imagined what would it be like to play with them? Maybe one day there'd be a poster of me playing for United. Imagine that! I thought about what it would be like to play in front of 76,000 fans.

At last I fell fast asleep and dreamed. In my dream I was playing at Old Trafford. I wore my number seven shirt. I could hear the roar of the crowd. I was the star player. I scored a hat trick. They gave me the match ball. But when I woke up I was still a nine-year-old kid who had to go to school.

I had a second trial the next week. All day in
school I couldn't think about anything else. The
teacher told me off for day-dreaming. I didn't
care. I went to school every day. It wasn't every
day you had a trial for Manchester United.

Dad drove me to the trial that afternoon. As we got out of the car he had a word with me.

"Forget the scout," he said. "Just show me what you can do."

I laughed.

"That's what Georgie said," I told him.

"Georgie?" Dad asked. "Georgie who?"

I didn't know how to explain.

"Forget it," I said.

The trial went well, better than the first one. I wasn't as nervous and everything I tried came off. This time I knew I was the best player.

The club asked Dad if he wanted to sign schoolboy forms. Dad said yes, of course.

The letter saying I could start at the Man U Academy came a few days later. Mum put it in a frame.

Chapter 3
Jimmy and Bryan

So I joined the under-10s at the Manchester United Academy. Most big football clubs have an Academy. It's where they train up young players to play for them once they're old enough.

I had to work hard. There was training three days a week after school. I enjoyed training. There was always something new to learn. But the best bit was Sunday morning. That's when there was a proper competition match. That's what football's all about. Every Sunday we played against another professional club's Academy side.

The first time I played for my new team I really wanted to do well. I kept calling for the ball. Sometimes I got it. More often I didn't. That was annoying. How could I score if I didn't have the ball? When I didn't get the pass, I chased after it and got it myself.

Once, I was a bit too keen. I pushed another member of our team off the ball. It was the wrong thing to do but I didn't care. I was a better player than him. Everyone said so. Next minute, I heard people shouting at me. But I took no notice. I only had one thought in my mind. I sprinted down the wing and beat two boys. When I broke into the penalty area, I shot. It nearly broke the net. I ran the length of the field with my arms raised. I was the star player this time.

But the coach had other ideas. He didn't think I was the star player at all. He thought I was selfish. When the whistle blew, he called me over.

"How do you think you did?" he asked.

"I scored," I said. "Didn't you see that goal?"

"I saw it," he said. "But we lost the game 2–1. You were too greedy. You were playing for yourself. You should be playing for the team."

I couldn't understand why he wasn't happy.
I beat two players. I scored. What more did he
want? It wasn't my fault the rest of the team
played badly. I walked off on my own with
my head down. I was in a bad mood all day.
There was only one man I could ask about the
game. That was Bryan Robson, one of United's
greatest captains.

Bryan said I only cared about myself. I scored but the team lost, and football's a team game. Everything I did had to be for the team.

I got picked again the next Sunday. It was the local derby against Manchester City under-10s. This time I knew I was playing to stay in the team. The coaching staff were watching me. They wanted to see what I'd do. I already knew. It's no good being selfish. The team is bigger than any one player.

City were good. They went 2–1 up. This time I didn't hog the ball. I passed to the other players. I made runs into the box. I played for the team.

First, I laid on the equaliser. Then I won the penalty that would put us in the lead. I think some of the boys expected me to grab the ball and take the penalty myself. But I'd learned my lesson. A boy called Chris takes our penalties. I handed the ball to him and he scored.

I scored twice after that. We won 5–3 in the end. But that wasn't the best bit. The coach came over and told me I'd done well.

"Today you turned into a team player," he said. "We've been looking for someone to be captain. I think I've just found him."

Next Sunday I wore the captain's armband.
I was so proud.

Bryan Robson
Captain Fantastic

⚽ Bryan Robson was born on 11th January, 1957 in the North East of England.

⚽ He became captain of Manchester United and England.

⚽ He scored 99 goals in 437 games.

⚽ He is the only British captain to lead a side to three FA Cup wins.

⚽ He won the League Championship with United in 1993 and 1994.

⚽ He won the 1991 European Cup Winners Cup with United.

Chapter 4
Jimmy and Eric

Every season, the club looks at the boys in each year group. They release five or six players. The coaches take you to one side. They tell you that you aren't going to make it. I thought I'd done well but I was a bit worried.

At the end of the first year, the club sent a written report on my progress.

Mum and Dad read it then handed it to me. I could hardly look.

This is what it said –

Ball Skills

Control: Very good.

Passing: Very good.
He must learn how to pass with both feet.

Stamina: Very good.

Strength: Very good.

Speed: Very good.

Team Play

Positional sense: Very good. Being made captain has helped his game.

Attitude: Jimmy can sometimes be selfish. Being captain has improved his team play. He works hard and listens to the coaches (most of the time). He has great motivation. He is a natural goal-scorer. His football skills are excellent. Keep it up!

I didn't like that stuff about being selfish. I'd worked on that. I wasn't sure if it was a good report or not. I didn't want the club to let me go.

Then I got the news. The coaches thought I'd done well. They wanted me back for another year. That wasn't all. They put me in the under-12s and I wasn't 11 yet!

But that season I had another problem. I was younger than the other boys. Some of the players who marked me were really strong. One day there was a boy who wasn't just strong. He was dirty. He couldn't keep up with me so he kept on fouling. Every time I got the ball he kicked me. I wanted the referee to do something. He took no notice. Then we got a corner. I went up for it and tried to head the ball. My marker tugged my shirt and I fell. I got up and shouted for a penalty. The referee shook his head.

Well, that was it. I ran after him shouting. He told me to calm down but I couldn't get over it. I knew I was right so I just kept shouting. Then I saw the boy who had pulled my shirt and I pushed him. He fell down as if he'd been shot.

They don't send you off for bad behaviour at the Academy the way they do in a proper game. They just decide you've lost it and so they put someone else on. There's no punishment afterwards. When they took me off, I saw the boy laughing.

That's when I really saw red. I pulled my boots off and threw them on the ground.

The coaches weren't happy.

"Don't do that again," they said. "You've got to control yourself."

I couldn't handle it. It wasn't my fault. The boy fouled me.

A few days later I found out I was going to be substitute in the next game. I'd lost my place because of my bad temper.

There was only one thing to do, ask my heroes. I knew a player who'd got into trouble then re-started his career. He once jumped into the crowd and kicked a fan. That got him banned for months. Even after that, he returned to play for Manchester United. He was Eric Cantona.

Eric said I had to stay cool. I had to wait for my chance and come back even stronger.

They didn't play me for two games. It was killing me sitting on the bench watching the other boys. Then, at half time in the second game, the coaches told me to get ready. I was a bit rusty at first. My touch wasn't right. But I kept going and got into the game. Soon I started to play better and I hit the post with a great shot.

The boy I was up against was too slow to catch me. I set up the next goal and scored one myself. Because he couldn't keep up with me, the boy tripped me. I crashed to the ground and it knocked the wind out of me. The boy tripped me again five minutes later.

I knew the coaches were watching me and I didn't get angry. I got better. I skipped over the lad's next tackle then I ran onto the ball and lobbed the keeper. I knew it was a good goal. Maybe it was the best I'd ever scored. Everyone stood and clapped. I smiled to myself. I was back.

Eric Cantona
Eric the King

⚽ Eric Cantona was born on 24th May, 1966 in Paris, France and grew up in Marseille.

⚽ He scored 82 goals for United in 184 games.

⚽ When he joined United, they won the league title for the first time in 26 years.

⚽ He won the Premier League four times and the FA Cup twice.

⚽ In 1995 a fan was shouting abuse at him. Eric lost his temper and gave the fan a Kung Fu kick. He was banned from playing football for the rest of the season.

⚽ He scored in his first match back with United.

⚽ Fans at United still sing his name and carry French flags.

Chapter 5
Jimmy and David

I'm fourteen now. Things are starting to get serious. I've been with the Academy for five years. The training has gone up from three nights a week to four.

There's an overseas competition this year. If I get picked, I'm going to Germany. There's a trophy at the end of it. I'm desperate to go. Every boy who gets in the team is closer to his dream. One day he might make it as a professional footballer.

My game has improved a lot. I share all the dead ball kicks with Chris, the boy I told you about before. But I don't share penalties – Chris still takes them. I've scored a few goals from free kicks this year. It's a big part of my game.

We played Liverpool today. That's a big game for us. There's always a lot of competition between the two teams. I knew I had to perform well to make sure I go to Germany.

It was a tough game, harder than most. They scored first. We equalised then Chris scored one of his penalties to put us in front. Liverpool squared it at 2–2 just before the end. I think I played all right but I didn't score.

Now I'm sitting in the changing rooms waiting to hear if I'm going to Germany. The coaches walk in and pin a team sheet on the notice board. Everyone crowds round it but I wait at the back. I daren't look. When most people have drifted off, I go and look.

I'm in!

It's exciting going abroad to play but everyone's waiting for the first match. We win easily. We win the second match too. That means we're playing the Dutch team Ajax in the semi-final. They have a really good Academy. Their young players are among the best in Europe. We'll have to be at the top of our game for this one.

It starts badly. Our centre half scores an own goal after ten minutes. It gets even worse just before half time when Ajax score again. Their striker skips past our defence like we're just not there. We're 2–0 down at half time and we sit in silence. Our heads are down. The coaches do their best to get our minds right but I'm not sure it's working. I do the old trick again. I know who I have to talk to.

****

Beckham tells me not to rush things. Keep on playing. Help your team mates by setting an example. You can still get back into a game, even in the last few minutes. Beckham did it for United in the Champions League Final against Bayern Munich. He did it for England in the European Championship against Greece. I can do it for my team.

In the second half I chase every ball. I start making runs and putting Ajax under pressure. For the first time they're not coming at us. Chris sees that I'm having an effect and then he starts to fight for every ball.

Before long, we are getting into the game. Possession is 50–50. But we can't score. Twice I sky the ball over the bar. Chris hits the post. At least we're attacking.

There's only ten minutes left and I don't know how the game's going to finish. Are we going to get back into the match?

I see Chris free on the right and cross the ball. He hits it back across the box on the volley. I only have to get a touch and it will fly in. I throw myself at it. I'm gutted when I kick thin air. But their full back has tried to get at the ball too and it flies into the net off his knee. Their net.

It's an own goal and it's all down to the pressure I put on their defence.

Ajax rally and the game flows from end to end. We stung them with that last goal and they're trying to put the game out of our reach. But that's the wrong thing to do. If they keep the game tight they will probably hang on to their lead. But they're leaving lots of gaps that we can run into. We just have to keep going.

Everyone's tired. I have to force myself to run. At last I get my second wind. Soon I seem to be covering every blade of grass as I keep after the ball. With a minute to go it pays off. Their captain has his foot too high and catches me in the face. It hurts but I've won a free kick on the edge of the area.

I shake away the pain and place the ball. Their keeper is trying to get the wall right but one of the defenders isn't listening. He's left a gap. I remember that Beckham free kick for England against Greece, and curl my foot round

the ball. It flies through the gap in the wall,
past the keeper's fingertips and into the net.

2–2.

The game goes to a penalty shoot-out. I
take the first one and score. Their first penalty
taker misses. After that, we score every
penalty. So do Ajax. In the end, our penalty

expert Chris only has to score and we've done it, we're through. Chris keeps a cool head and does his job. He sends the keeper the wrong way.

We're in the final!

David Beckham
Free Kick Master

⚽ David Beckham was born on May 2nd, 1975.

⚽ He became World Player of the Year in 1999.

⚽ He is the only Englishman to score in three different World Cups.

⚽ He helped Manchester United be the top Premier League club in the 1990s.

⚽ He won the treble of League, FA Cup and Champions League in 1999.

⚽ In August 1996 he scored from the halfway line against Wimbledon.

⚽ In the 1998 World Cup he was sent off after kicking Argentina's Diego Simeone. A hate campaign followed because England were knocked out. This was mostly in the press but some fans booed him as well. But David Beckham got over it. Soon he was one of the most popular players in England once more.

Chapter 6
Jimmy and Cristiano

In the final our team plays the home team, Bayern Munich. This time there's no big problem for me. I haven't made any mistakes. But it's time to use everything I ever learned.

I go through my lessons. *Keep your mind on the game and nothing else. Play for the team. Control your temper. Play to the very end of every match.* I have a quick word with one of my favourite number sevens, Cristiano Ronaldo.

He tells me to express myself and just play my game. If I have the skill and the right attitude, it will show on the pitch.

I'm nervous at kick-off but I don't try too hard. I play my normal game. I make runs. I find space. I spray passes to my teammates. I feel good. Everything I do feels so natural.

Bayern Munich score first from a corner. It's a set-back but our heads don't go down. We carry on playing. Just before half-time Chris beats his man and whips in a low cross. I meet it with my head and it loops over the keeper and into the net.

1–1.

After half-time home advantage starts to tell. Bayern are on top and I have to help with the defending. Bayern keep pressing and go back into the lead with a cracking goal. It could be worse but I clear the ball off the goal line from a corner.

At least they are only 2–1 up. It isn't much to show after all the pressing they have done. We're losing but we're still in the game.

With ten minutes left, I pick up the ball on the half-way line. The Bayern Munich lads are getting tired and they're giving me too much space. I go on a run and leave two of their players for dead. I've been running myself into the ground. A few minutes ago I was panting like a dog. Funny thing, I don't feel tired any more. I'm getting stronger.

I skip past another player and pass to Chris. He rolls it back to me as I run on and I stroke it into the net under the keeper's body.

2–2.

It's Bayern's turn to fall back. They're defending really deep. Every time we attack, they sky the ball, or kick it out of play. The midfield players aren't passing well. They panic a lot. It shows they're really tired.

We take advantage. With just five minutes to go, I break into the penalty area and hit the ball into the top corner. We're winning 3–2. As long as we don't do anything stupid, the trophy is ours.

Bayern try to go forward but their moves keep breaking down. The ref is looking at his watch when I see Chris making a run. I pick

him out with a long pass. He skips past their
keeper and slots the ball home.

It's 4–2. They won't come back from this.

A minute later the whistle goes. We've won the trophy.

When we land at Manchester Airport Mum and Dad are waiting. The coach tells me I've got a bright future.

"You've done well," he says.

"I had a lot of help," I tell him.

Mum and Dad think I mean the coaching staff. The coach thinks I mean my parents. They're both right. But there are some other people to thank.

Cristiano Ronaldo
There's only one Ronaldo

⚽ Cristiano Ronaldo was born in Portugal on February 5th, 1985.

⚽ On 29th October 2005 he scored Manchester United's 1,000th Premiership goal.

⚽ He was the FIFPro Special Young Player of the Year in 2005.

⚽ Cristiano Ronaldo helped United win the Premiership title in 2007, 2008 and 2009, and the UEFA Champions League in 2008.

⚽ He scored a total of 118 goals for Manchester United.

⚽ In 2009 Ronaldo was named FIFA World Player of the Year.

⚽ He was transferred for a record fee of £80 million to Real Madrid in July 2009.

Our books are tested
for children and young people by
children and young people.

Thanks to everyone who consulted on
a manuscript for their time and effort in
helping us to make our books better
for our readers.